Josie's
Shiny
Key

Trilogy Christian Publishers
A Wholly Owned Subsidary of Trinity Broadcasting Network
2442 Michelle Drive
Tustin, CA 92780

For information, address Trilogy Christian Publishing
Rights Department, 2442 Michelle Drive, Tustin, Ca 92780.
Trilogy Christian Publishing/ TBN and colophon are trademarks of Trinity Broadcasting Network.

For information about special discounts for bulk purchases, please contact Trilogy Christian Publishing.

Manufactured in the United States of America

Trilogy Disclaimer: The views and content expressed in this book are those of the author and may not necessarily reflect the views and doctrine of Trilogy Christian Publishing or the Trinity Broadcasting Network.

10 9 8 7 6 5 4 3 2 1

Library of Congress Cataloging-in-Publication Data is available.

ISBN 978-1-64773-544-9 (Print Book)
ISBN 978-1-64773-545-6 (ebook)

Josie's Shiny Key

JOAN ELLEN CAMP

1

Josie's spunky personality was infectious. You couldn't help but catch the joy that radiated from her when she entered the room. Her sassy style wasn't complete until brilliant colored ribbons were cleverly woven through her long, golden brown braids. Her cornflower blue eyes joyfully twinkled, and her fingernails, well, were always painted a color wheel of colors.

"Aren't they perfect?" she'd ask, as she wiggled her little painted masterpieces. Her mom always said that God had blessed Josie with an illuminating spirit and a kind soul.

"Honey, let that sunny spirit of yours shine bright, and you'll make a difference in this world. You have a loving heart that can turn an ordinary day into an extraordinary day and raindrops into rainbows. Pay attention and use these gifts that you've been given to help others, and you'll be the one that truly benefits. You'll see!"

Josie's life changed a lot this past year, in marvelous ways, after her mom gave her a special gift—a gift that could help her display *her very own gift* for all to see.

The key that hung around Josie's neck and over her heart was shiny and in the shape of a cross, safely fastened to a pink and lime green striped rope that her mom had gotten her over the summer at a neighborhood yard sale.

4

"That's just perfect!" she told her mother. In fact, Josie always said, "Everything in life is just perfect, the way it's supposed to be!"

Each morning, without fail, she'd grab her shiny key and colorful diary from the night stand, ready to capture the events of the day, and jot 'em down. "Keepin' tabs!" she'd say.

But first, she'd slip on her colorful tutu, put her well used stubby pencil into the front pocket and her special embroidered handkerchief into the back pocket, before heading downstairs to greet her mom and dad with a good morning hug.

Before running down, she'd stop at the top of the stairs and smile as she read the words that she had securely taped to the cover of her cherished diary. "God, can You read human words? Yes, I believe You can!" she'd boldly say.

8

Josie loved everything about school, especially art and creative writing! One morning, just before the first bell rang, as she confidently walked to class running her stubby pencil eraser along the row of bright orange lockers, Josie saw Liam struggling to open his locker door. She noticed from a distance that he'd gotten an awesome buzz cut, was wearing his favorite red Converse sneakers, and, as usual, proudly wore his big, black glasses. Liam and Josie share the same birthday, are the best of friends, and will both be turning eight in a few short months. Unlike Josie though, Liam enjoys science. "There's a logical reason for everything," he'd say. But that morning, she could tell that he was super frustrated. She calmly walked up to him and said, "Excuse me, Liam," ever so politely. "I see you're struggling to open your locker." "Yep!" he growled.

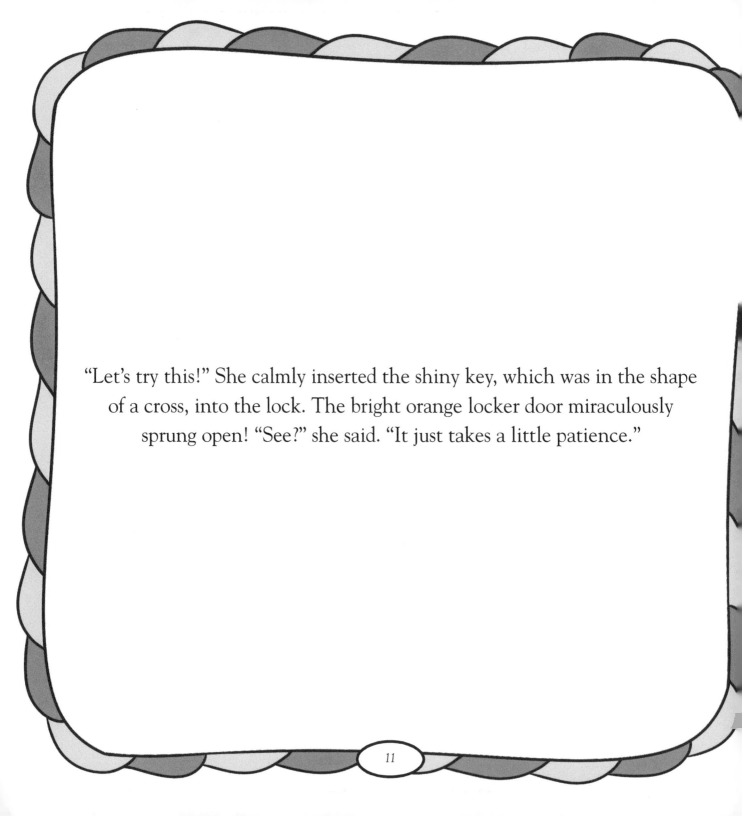

"Let's try this!" She calmly inserted the shiny key, which was in the shape of a cross, into the lock. The bright orange locker door miraculously sprung open! "See?" she said. "It just takes a little patience."

Liam jumped up with excitement! "Thank you so much, Josie! You helped me out just in the nick of time! High five!" Josie high fived her friend with a smirk, then they happily skipped off to class. "I guess some things can't be explained!" he grinned.

Later that school year, as she joyfully skipped home, the key wildly swinging beneath her jacket and over her heart, Josie abruptly stopped in her tracks! She noticed a sweet old lady standing there with a bewildered stare, in front of her bright red, paint chipped front door. The old lady had snowy white hair worn in a tidy bun. Her reusable grocery bag was huge with bright colored tropical birds on it and was overflowing with groceries.

Josie cautiously walked up the old lady's cracked sidewalk and kindly asked, "May I help you?" "I can't open my door! This has never happened to me before. It's stuck! I don't know what to do! What would you do?" Josie knew exactly what to do.

16

"Let's try this!" She thoughtfully inserted the shiny key, which was in the shape of a cross, into the lock of the old lady's bright red, paint chipped front door, and it opened with a creak. She stepped back, making room for the sweet old lady to go inside. "There." Josie quietly whispered, "It just takes a little kindness." The sweet old lady was thrilled! Her tiny eyes twinkled with joy as she invited Josie to stay for some cookies and milk.

"You're such a kind girl. Thank you so much for noticing that I needed help." Josie smiled, then declined respectfully and waved as she continued skipping home. It wasn't until that evening that she realized she never got that sweet old lady's name.

Josie had many wonderful stories that she'd jotted in her colorful diary. She would tell her friends, "I believe that everyday is a gift when you do the right thing with what ya have. I wear my shiny key and carry my colorful diary to be prepared. You never know when they might come in handy!" she smiled brightly! In fact, she shared with her friends a meaningful experience that had taken place recently and how happy she was that she had a chance to help her special friend and neighbor.

It was a beautiful Saturday morning. Of course,
to Josie, everyday was a beautiful day.

She was relaxed and quite content, lounging on her front
porch daydreaming a little and jottin' a lot, fillin' page
after page with her thoughts and fun experiences.

Josie eventually looked up and noticed several cars had gathered at her neighbor's house. She jumped off her weathered blue porch, missing the bottom step altogether, then snuck over straight away, peeking through the beautifully manicured bushes that bordered their driveways. To Josie's surprise, her friend Beatrice was sitting alone on her porch swing, crying uncontrollably. Beatrice had funky, curly red hair, tiny freckles, the greenest green eyes, and was always so happy-go-lucky. That day, her red hair seemed to glow in the morning sun, but her tears were not so happy-go-lucky.

Josie joined her on the swing and asked with concern, "What's wrong? Why are you crying? Why so many cars?" Her friend cried out, "My daddy got hurt at work and was taken to the hospital! I'm worried, and now... I can't open my old green metal box. I've tried and tried! It's filled with special things he's given me!" Josie wiped her friends' tears with her special embroidered handkerchief that she faithfully carried in her back pocket as they both looked down at the old green metal box. "I'm sad and very scared!" Beatrice sobbed. Josie thought for a moment about how important this was.

With a soothing voice, she said, "Beatrice, let's try this." Josie lovingly inserted the shiny key, which was in the shape of a cross, into the lock of her friends' old green metal box. It easily opened. Joyfully, but to herself, Josie said, "It just takes a little love."

On top of the many small treasures that were safely hidden in the old green metal box was a handwritten note the little girl's dad had placed there.

It read, "Honey, do your best to be patient, kind, and loving. Remember that the cross is the key to living a happy, fulfilled, and meaningful life. Through God's grace, you can help calm the frustrated with patience, help someone in need with kindness, and help those who are afraid with love. Love, Dad"

Josie's eyes filled with big, thick tears. She held onto the key that hung around her neck and over her heart, which was shiny and in the shape of a cross, safely fastened to a pink and lime green striped rope. At that moment, sitting next to her dear friend, Josie bowed her head. She quietly whispered, "Thank You, Father God, for giving me the key." Beatrice leaned in for a hug, and her green eyes once again shined with joy.

That night Josie carefully laid her special embroidered handkerchief, stubby pencil and colorful diary on her night stand as she did every night. With a sincere belief in her heart, feeling loved, comforted, and extremely satisfied, she closed her sleepy eyes and said a little prayer, as her mom stood nearby and quietly listened.

"Father God, I thank You for showing me that I've always had the key. It's a special gift from You that lives deep in my heart. It's shiny and bright, and it shines the most when I'm helping others."

"And that's perfect!"

Let your light shine before men, that they may see *your* good works, and glorify *your* Father which is in heaven.
Matthew 5:16 KJV

What are "your" special God-given gifts and talents?

_____

_____

_____

_____

_____

_____

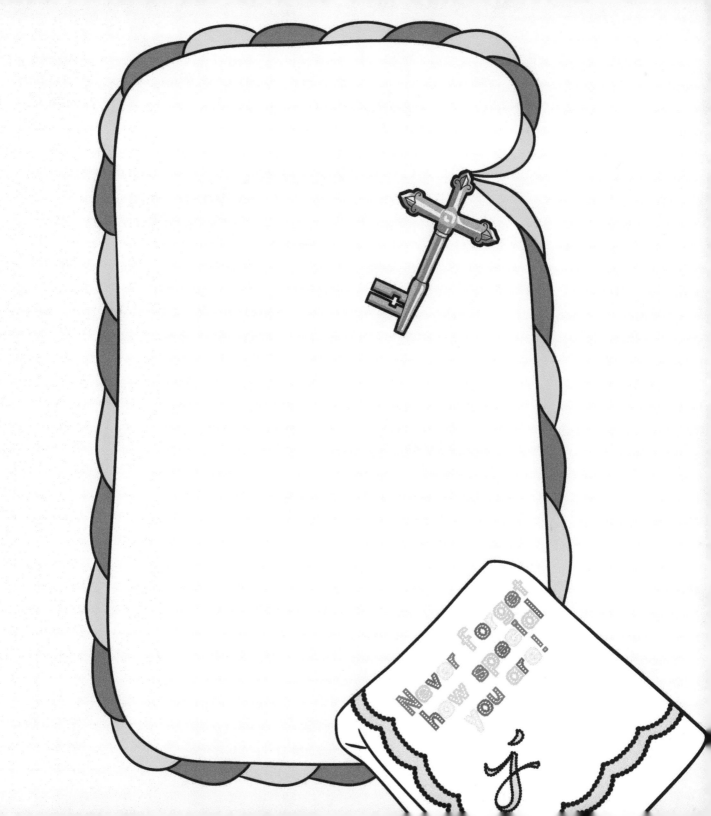

Never forget how speal you are

j

CPSIA information can be obtained
at www.ICGtesting.com
Printed in the USA
BVHW051400220421
605637BV00012B/1812

9 781647 735449